THIS WALKER BOOK BELONGS TO:

JET CAR – RACING CAR

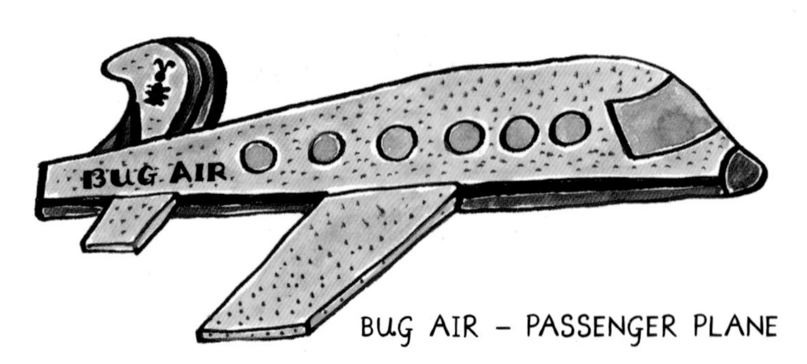

BUG AIR – PASSENGER PLANE

THE NATIONAL – STEAM ENGINE

POLICE CAR (FRENCH)

ROCKET EXPRESS – STEAM TRAIN

BATH BOY – DIESEL TRAIN

FLEUR – STEAM ENGINE

THE LITTLE LEANER – DIESEL TRAIN

LOGO RACING CAR

HACKNEY EXPRESS

SUPER STAR JET ENGINE – JET PLANE

SMALL CAR WITH SUNROOF

N°17 RALLY RACER

LITTLE STAR – DIESEL ENGINE

DOUBLE CRANE TRAIN

1 2 3 – SHORTHAUL PLANE

Nº8 RALLY RACER WITH BOOT

MINI CAR

SUPER STUNT – STUNT PLANE

LUXURY VINTAGE CAR

– DIESEL TRAIN

Nº5 OPEN-TOP RACING CAR

LITTLE LOGO – STEAM ENGINE

LITTLE STUNT CAR

SOFT-TOP CAR

SILVERLINK SILVERDREAM RACER – DIESEL TRAIN

FLOWER BEETLE CAR

First published 2006 by Walker Books Ltd
87 Vauxhall Walk, London SE11 5HJ

10 9 8 7 6 5 4 3 2 1

This book has been typeset in LNSpanyolSemiBold

Printed in China

British Library Cataloguing in Publication Data:
a catalogue record for this book is available from the British Library

ISBN-13: 978-1-4063-0371-1

www.walkerbooks.co.uk

Go Bugs Go!

Jessica Spanyol

WALKER BOOKS
AND SUBSIDIARIES
LONDON • BOSTON • SYDNEY • AUCKLAND

Good Morning, Bugs

Come and meet the Bugs.

This is Bob.
Good morning,
Bob.

This is Clemence.
Good morning,
Clemence.

This is Tate.
Good morning,
Tate.

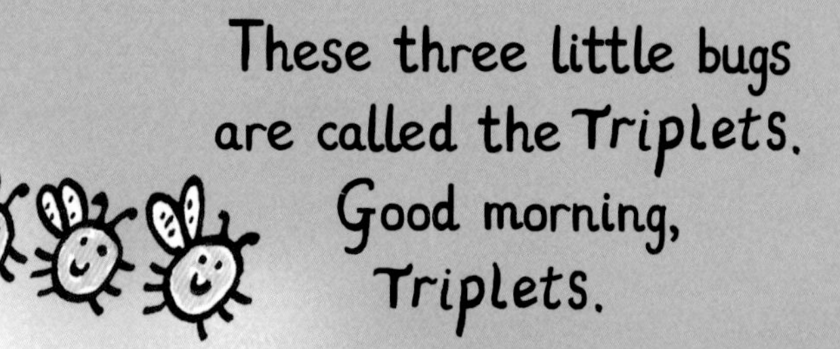

These three little bugs
are called the Triplets.
Good morning,
Triplets.

And here's *Stacie*,
carrying lots of shopping bags.
Good morning,
Stacie.

This is Giorgio.
Good morning,
Giorgio.

This is Keith,
drinking a cup of tea.
Good morning,
Keith.

This is Jo-Jo.
Jo-Jo really likes flowers.
Good morning,
Jo-Jo.

Here's **Mr Thornton-Jones**.
He's got glasses and lots
and lots of friends.
Good morning,
Mr Thornton-Jones
and friends.

And this is Pauline and the girls.
Good morning,
Pauline and the girls.

All the **Bugs** really like driving. Today they are looking forward to having lots of fun with their trains, cars and planes.

Come on, Bugs, let's have some fun!

Ready, Steady, Oops!

Here are all the **Bugs** in their racing cars, getting ready to play Ready, Steady, Oops!

Tate's Nº2 vintage racing car is quite old. Sometimes the front wheel comes off.

Bob's Nº1 streamlined racer can go really fast.

Vroom!
Vroom!

Clemence is in his logo racing car.

The Triplets' little rally racer has a new engine in it.

Vroom!
Vroom!

Keith is in his Jet Car and he has a cup of milk.

Vroom! Vroom!

Mr Thornton-Jones' Nº9 racing car has a tail to help it go faster.

Vroom! Vroom!

Stacie's Nº8 rally racer has a boot that lifts up.

Vroom! Vroom!

Jo-Jo is in her Nº17 rally racer.

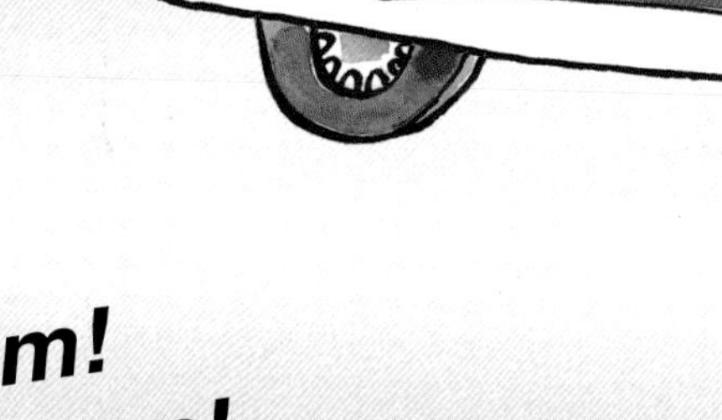

Vroom! Vroom!

Pauline and the girls are in their open-top star car.

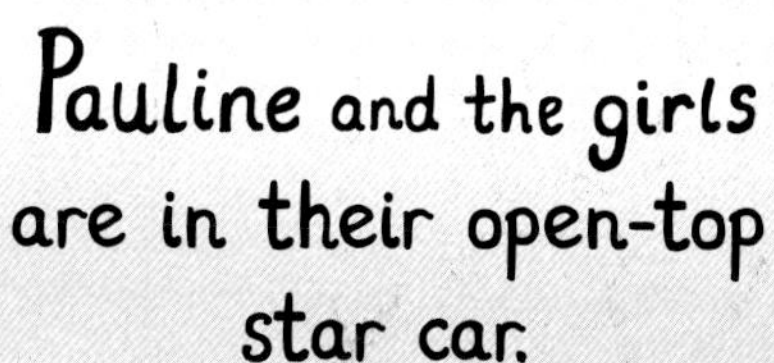

Vroom! Vroom!

Giorgio has a big bottle of water in the back of his Nº5 open-top racing car.

Ready, steady ...

OOPS!
"Yippee!"
"Again, again!"
"Whee!"
"OOPS! I've been bashed!"
"OOPS! There goes my wheel!"
Bash!
"OOPS! I've lost control!"
"OOPS! Sorry, Keith!"
Jet car
Bump!

"OOPS! My glasses!"
"Whee! We love this!"
"OOPS! My boot's come open!"
"OOPS! OK, girls?"
Bash!
"OOPS! Look at me! I'm flying!"
"OOPS! This is great fun!"
"OOPS! There goes my water!"
Bump!
Bash!

Singing on the Trains

Now all the **Bugs** are in their diesel trains. They love to sing and hoot as they chug along. All together now, all join in.

The hooters on the trains go hoot hoot hoot,
hoot hoot hoot, hoot hoot hoot.
The hooters on the trains go hoot hoot hoot,
all day long.

Mr Thornton-Jones likes to do lots of little hoots.

Hoot hoot hoot hoot hoot hoot!

Tate's train makes a gentle hooting sound.

Hoot hoot hoot!

Bob's hooter is very loud.

HOOT!

Clemence is an expert hooter.
Hoot hoot hoot!
Royal Express
15412
Pauline is good at hooting too.
Hoot hoot hoot!
The flyer
Giorgio has two hooters on his train.
Hoot hoot!
Hoot hoot!
HACKNEY EXPRESS
The Triplets all take turns to hoot.
Hoot!
Hoot!
Hoot!
1 2 3
Jo-Jo's train is only little, but it's got a big hooter.
Hoot!
Glasgow flower
Keith likes hooting very much.
Hoot hoot hoot hoot!
SSR
Silverlink Silverdream Racer
Stacie likes to do long, loud hoots!
Hooot hoooot hoooot!
Classy girl
6789

Jumbo
Jet
Ready, Steady, Take Off!
Here are the Bugs, zooming down the runway in their jumbo jet. Mr Thornton-Jones and friends have missed the plane and are trying to catch up.
Clemence's favourite seat is at the back.
The Triplets love looking out of the window as they zoom along.
Giorgio is going to have a turn flying the plane next.
Pauline and the girls love flying.
747
Zoom!
Zoom!
Zoom!

Bob can't wait for take off.

Jo-Jo loves the loud roar of the engines.

Tate always likes to sit at the front.

Stacie loves it when they lift off the runway.

Keith is the captain today. He is an excellent flyer.

Zoom!

Ready, steady...

Take Off!

Whoosh!

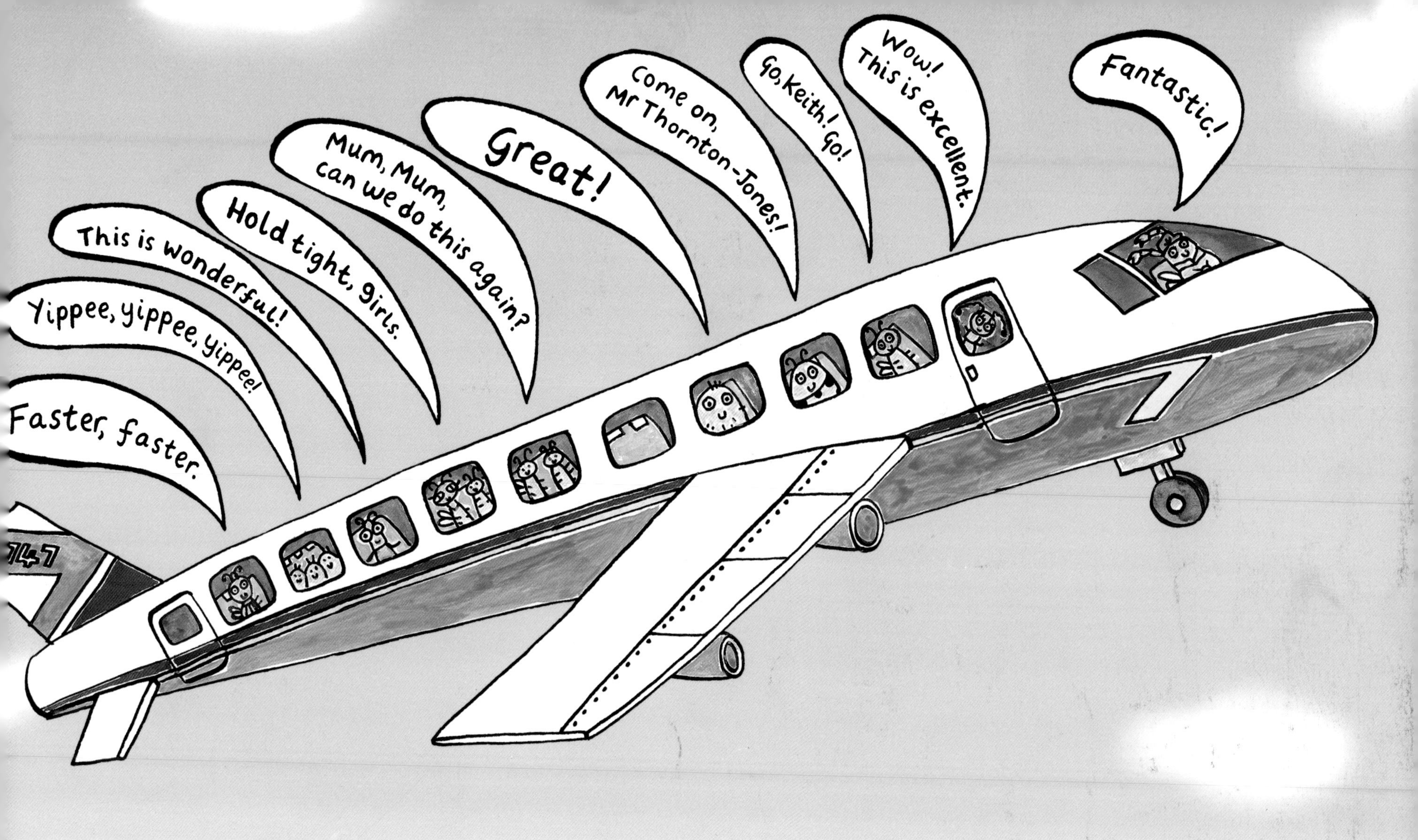
Faster, faster.
Yippee, yippee, yippee!
This is wonderful!
Hold tight, girls.
Mum, Mum, can we do this again?
Great!
Come on, Mr Thornton-Jones!
Go, Keith! Go!
Wow! This is excellent.
Fantastic!
747

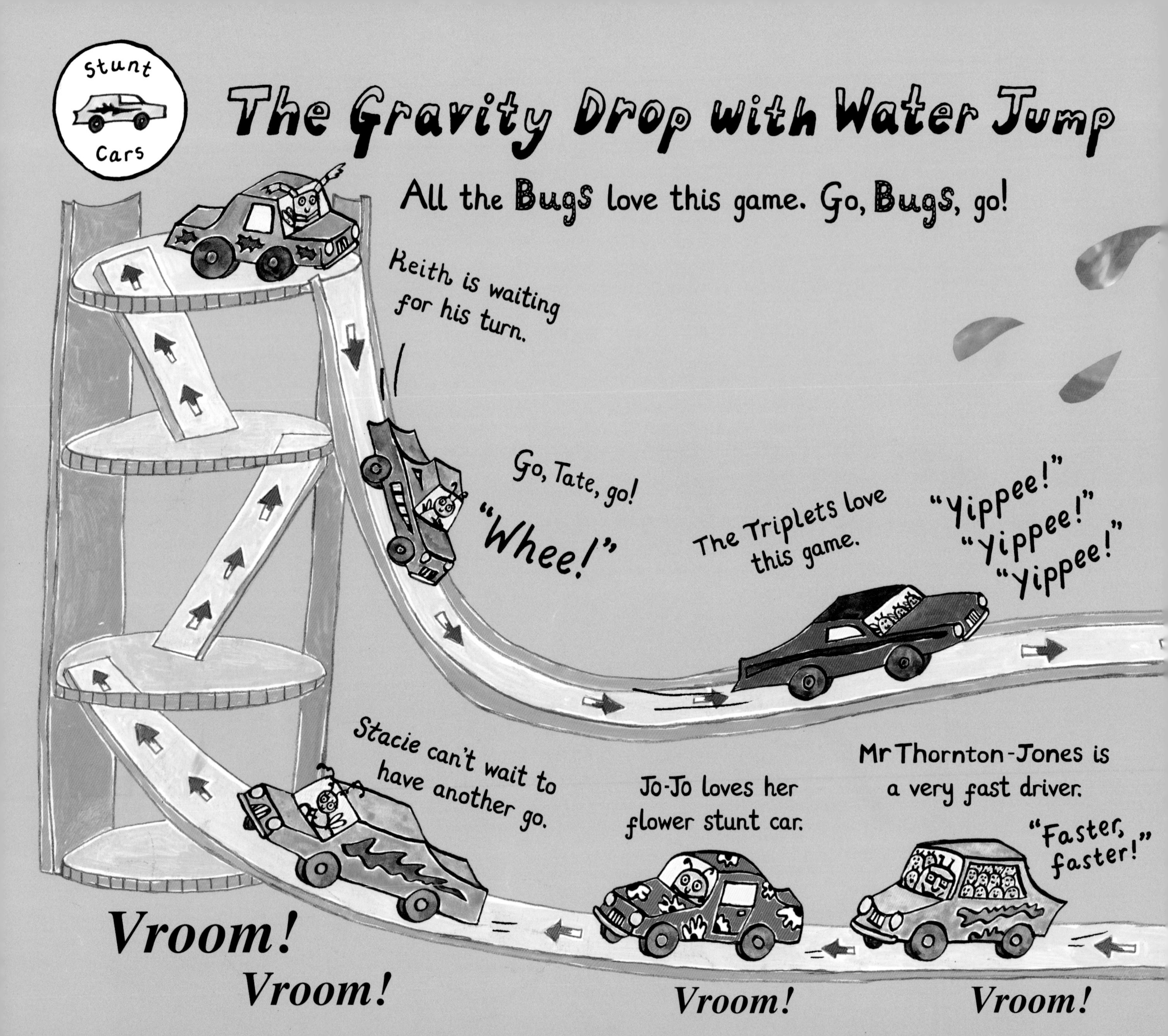
Stunt Cars
The Gravity Drop with Water Jump
All the Bugs love this game. Go, Bugs, go!
Keith is waiting for his turn.
Go, Tate, go!
"Whee!"
The Triplets love this game.
"Yippee!"
"Yippee!"
"Yippee!"
Stacie can't wait to have another go.
Jo-Jo loves her flower stunt car.
Mr Thornton-Jones is a very fast driver.
"Faster, faster!"
Vroom!
Vroom!
Vroom!
Vroom!

Clemence is an excellent fly driver!

"Whee!"

Bob loves sploshing in the water.

"Oops!"

Giorgio is in his little rescue truck.

"Oh no, not again, Bob!"

Pauline and the girls really like the Gravity Drop.

"Come on, girls, let's go round again."

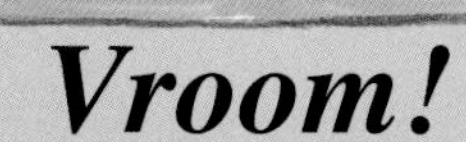

Vroom! Vroom!

Little Crashes

Look, the **Bugs** have had lots of little crashes.

Tate has bumped into Jo-Jo.

Jo-Jo really likes crashing and splashing.

The Triplets are in their super steam-powered propeller train and have bashed into Pauline and the girls.

Oops! Pauline and the girls have bumped into the back of *Stacie's* freight train.

Mr Thornton-Jones
and friends are in their
best engine. It's called
The Wild West.
"Whee!"
"Yikes!"
"Oi! get off our cowcatcher."
The Wild West
Bash!
Clemence has got stuck
on The Wild West's
cowcatcher.
Toot
tooooot!
Little Logo
"Hey, let me down!"

Stacie's train is called
The Little Lady.
It's her favourite
train.
"Who can help put
us back on the tracks?"
Toot toot tooooot!
Milk
The Little Lady
Bump!
Bash!

Here come the breakdown trains!

Mr Thornton-Jones and friends are pleased to see no damage has been done.

Clemence is very glad to be off the cowcatcher.

Bob's crane has a big, strong hook on it.

Keith has helped *Stacie* back onto the track and now Mr Thornton-Jones' friends are helping put some sugar back into her carriage and are checking over her train.

All better.

Fly, Bugs, Fly

Here are the **Bugs** in their aeroplanes. They love to sing as they fly along. All together now, all join in.

This is the way we fly our planes, fly our planes, fly our planes.
This is the way we fly our planes, on a cold and frosty morning.

Look, Bob's socks are fly-drying!

Pauline and the girls can do some great tricks!

Mr Thornton-Jones has lost his glasses again. Oops!

The white lines the planes make in the sky are called "contrails". *Stacie* loves making contrails.

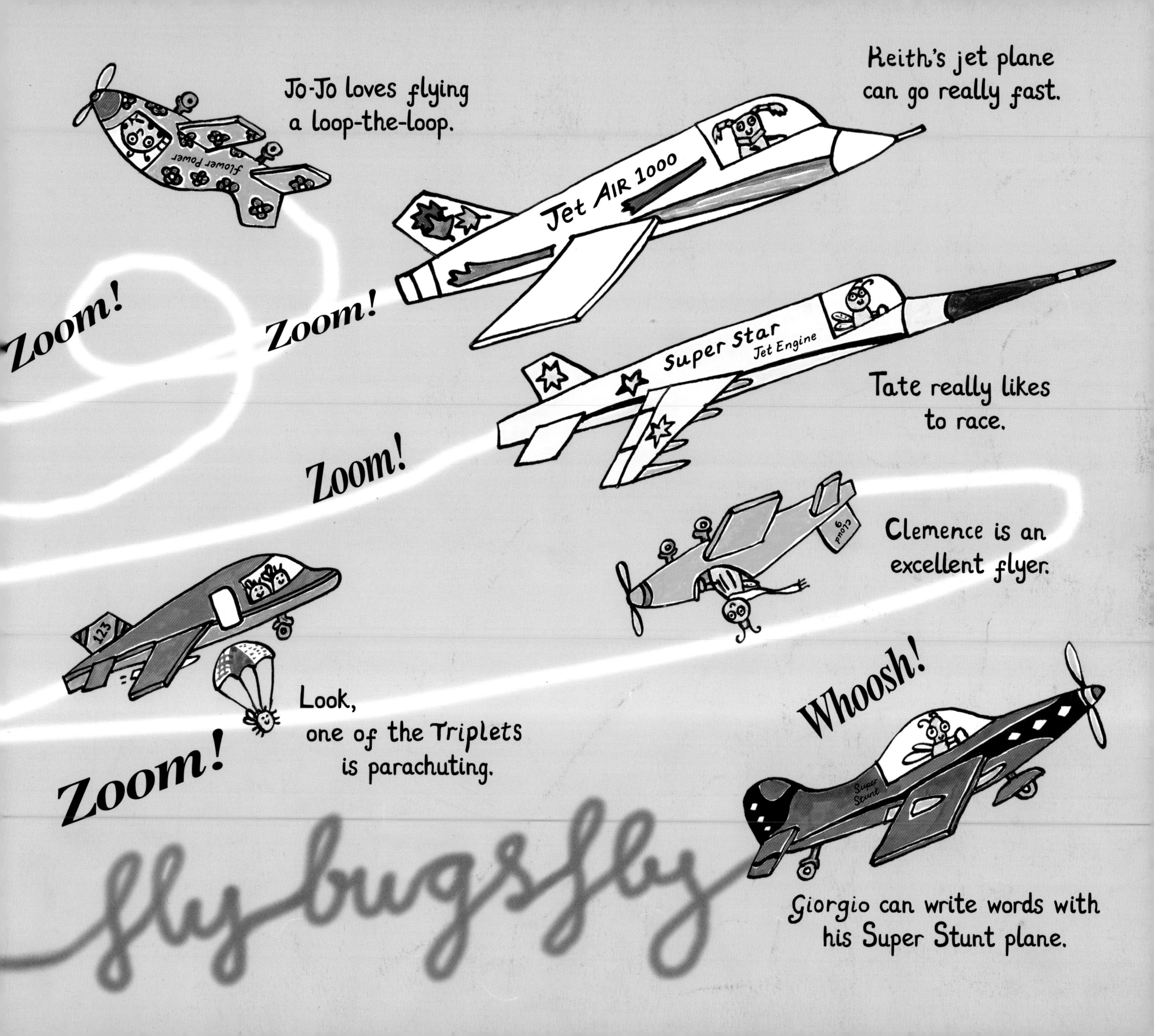
Jo-Jo loves flying
a loop-the-loop.
Flower Power
Keith's jet plane
can go really fast.
Jet AIR 1000
Zoom!
Zoom!
Super Star
Jet Engine
Tate really likes
to race.
Zoom!
Cloud 9
Clemence is an
excellent flyer.
123
Look,
one of the Triplets
is parachuting.
Zoom!
Whoosh!
Super Stunt
fly bugs fly
Giorgio can write words with
his Super Stunt plane.

Drive and Slide

Now, the **Bugs** are going to play **Drive and Slide**.
Along the road we go, up the ramp we go, and down we slide.

Mr Thornton-Jones and friends like making lots of noise in their police car.

Neenah neenah!

Neenah neenah!

Giorgio can't wait for his turn to slide.

Beep beeep!

Bob loves his little run-around-town car.

Pauline and the girls like going round and round on drive and slide.

Clemence is in his luxury vintage car.

Stacie is a very careful driver.

Keith's soft-top car can go ever so fast!

Tate is in his yellow mini car. Yellow is Tate's favourite colour.

Jo-Jo painted the flowers on her flower Beetle herself.

Hoot! Hoot!

The Triplets' luxury sports car is brand new.

Bye-Bye, Bugs

All the **Bugs** have had a lovely time with their planes, trains and cars, but now they have gone back home to put their feet up.

Bye-bye,
Mr Thornton-Jones
and friends.

Bye-bye,
Jo-Jo.

Bye-bye,
Tate.

Bye-bye,
Keith.

Bye-bye,
Giorgio.

Bye-bye,
Triplets.

Bye-bye, everyone.
See you again soon.

N°1 STREAMLINED RACER

RUN-AROUND-TOWN CAR

FLOWER POWER – PROPELLER PLANE

THE WILD WEST – STEAM ENGINE

THE FLYER – DIESEL TRAIN

CRANE TRAIN WITH HOOK

CLASSY GIRL

1 2 3 – INTERCITY DIESEL TRAIN

BOB 1 – LIGHT AIRCRAFT

1 2 3 GO! – PROPELLER TRAIN

ESTATE CAR WITH ROOF RACK

LUXURY SPORTS CAR

JET AIR 1000 – JET PLANE

ROYAL EXPRESS

FAMILY HATCHBACK

N°9 RACING CAR WITH TAIL

LITTLE RALLY RACER

CLOUD 9 – PROPELLER PLANE

– DIESEL TRAIN

GLASGOW FLOWER – DIESEL TRAIN

OPEN-TOP STAR CAR

GIRL POWER – PROPELLER PLANE

BREAKDOWN TRAIN WITH GRABBER

EXECUTIVE GIRL – JET STREAM PLANE

– DIESEL TRAIN

N°2 VINTAGE RACING CAR

THE LITTLE LADY – STEAM FREIGHT TRAIN